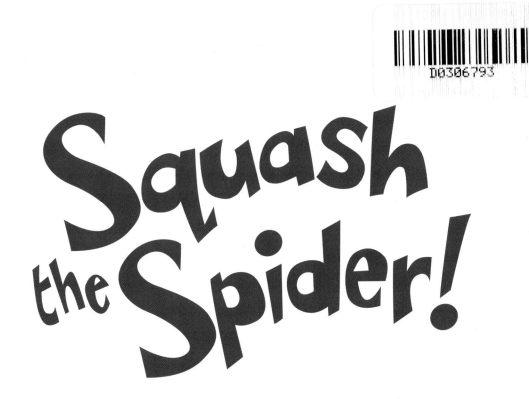

For Chris, Ian, Mark,
Richard and Roger.
Great with computers,
useless with spiders!

SQUASH THE SPIDER!
A PICTURE CORGI BOOK 9780552561754

First published in Great Britain by David Fickling Books,
an imprint of Random House Children's Books

David Fickling Books edition published 2003
Picture Corgi edition published 2004

3 5 7 9 10 8 6 4 2

Set in Esprit Book

Picture Corgi Books are published by Random House Children's Books,
61–63 Uxbridge Road, London W5 5SA,
a division of The Random House Group Ltd,
in Australia by Random House Australia (Pty) Ltd,
20 Alfred Street, Milsons Point, Sydney, NSW 2061, Australia,
in New Zealand by Random House New Zealand Ltd,
18 Poland Road, Glenfield, Auckland 10, New Zealand,
and in South Africa by Random House (Pty) Ltd,
Endulini, 5A Jubilee Road, Parktown 2193, South Africa

THE RANDOM HOUSE GROUP Limited Reg. No. 954009
www.**kids**at**randomhouse**.co.uk

A CIP catalogue record for this book is available from the British Library.

Printed in Singapore

Squash the Spider!

Nick Ward

Picture Corgi

High up on the ceiling Squash
the Spider was waiting to pounce!
Billy came in to watch T.V. and
eat his supper.

He settled in front of the telly.

Billy was just about to
take a great big bite out of
his sandwich when . . .

"Yuk!" screamed Billy. "Mum, **SQUASH the SPIDER!**"

But when Billy's mum rushed in, the spider was gone.

After supper it was Billy's bedtime.
"Goodnight Mum," he called. Billy
snuggled under his covers and was
soon fast asleep.
In a secret hiding place, Squash was
already snoring, dreaming up his
next trick.

At school the next day, Billy and his
friends sat down on the story mat.
"Ssh! Let's start with a nice quiet
story," whispered the teacher, opening
her book. "All about . . ."

A very noisy spider!

"Eek!" squealed the teacher.
"SQUASH the SPIDER!"

Squash jumped!
"Yuk!" cried the whole class.
"Where's he gone?"
But Squash had completely
disappeared!

At lunchtime, Billy was in the
playground with his friends.
"I'm not really scared of spiders,"
he explained. "I was only pretending."

"Me too," said Jo.
"Who wants a crisp?"
"What flavour?" asked Billy reaching into the bag.

"Yuk!" screamed Billy.
"SQUASH the SPIDER!"

Jo grabbed Squash. "I'm not scared,"
she said. "Look . . ."
Jo opened her fingers. Squash wriggled
his long spidery legs and . . .

Whizz! He shot straight up Jo's sleeve.

Yuk! Get him out!

Pop!

Jo wriggled and squiggled and flapped . . .

. . . And Squash flew out of Jo's other sleeve and tumbled to the ground.

Tee hee!

"Disgusting!"
Jo cried.
**"SQUASH
the SPIDER!"**

"Phew! That was close!" gasped Squash on the way home. "But I've learnt my lesson. I will never ever ever scare anyone again!"

"Promise?" asked Billy.

"Promise!" said Squash.

And from that day on, Squash the spider never shouted "Boo!" and never ever scared anyone again.

12

SPIDER LANE

Well, almost never.